A Christmas Tale

written by
Samuel R. Polakoff

illustrated by
Jennifer Taylor

This book is dedicated to my loving family and all others with the vision to help people to see.

Publisher: BookSurge
North Charleston, South Carolina
Library of Congress Control Number: 2007906099
ISBN Number: 1-4196-7572-9

Illustrations by Jennifer Taylor (www.jenniferlouisetaylor.com)

In a crowded section of downtown, on a cold, blustery Christmas Eve morning, Jack paced nervously across the dusty and barren floor. The windows were long gone in the abandoned apartment building where he was living with his family. The cold air sent a chill through his bones.

His two youngsters were hungry, as was his wife. None of them had eaten anything in a long time. Scavenging for food was becoming more challenging with each passing day. With Christmas approaching, Jack knew he would have nothing for his family. He barely had a roof overhead. He prayed for a warm and stable shelter with a modest amount of food for his family. Jack had just about given up hope.

At the same building, a young police officer arrived to investigate a reported disturbance. Officer Mark Monroe had been on the force for five years now. He was married with two small kids of his own. He and his wife had just moved into their first single family home on the outskirts of town. They had a little patch of lawn, just enough for a swing set and a teeter-totter for his two young daughters, ages 5 and 3. Officer Monroe was a good father and husband but he had one trait his wife, Julie, did not much care for. He was a procrastinator!

In Julie's family, the tradition for generations was that the parents buy the kids one present together and one special "surprise gift" from each parent. Mark knew that they had already taken care of their "together gift" for the kids and Julie had already purchased her surprise gift. Here he was on the day before Christmas without having figured out his own surprise gift for the girls. At that moment, he heard what he thought was a scratching noise coming from the first floor of the vacant building.

His attention was drawn completely back to the task at hand. Officer Monroe investigated carefully but found no evidence of anyone in the building, no disturbance, no comprehension at all as to why someone would have called this in. Officer Monroe was about to leave when Jack took note of his presence.

10

11

Feeling desperate and scared, Jack made his approach, hoping beyond hope that Officer Monroe might be the answer to his prayers. Mark looked down and saw a handsome, orange tabby rubbing up against his leg and purring like crazy. Mark had always loved cats, so he kneeled down to pet this homeless kitty. Jack was thrilled! This nice, young police officer had obviously taken a liking to him.

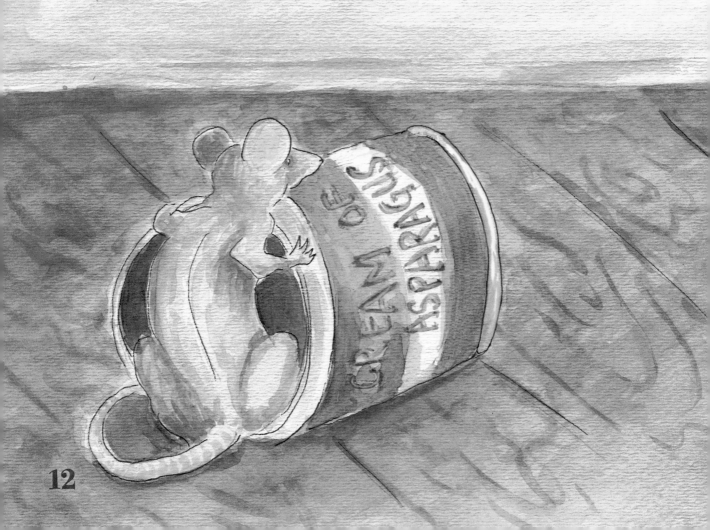

Jack meowed with all of the feeling he could muster and motioned Officer Monroe to follow him up the flight of stairs to the abandoned first floor. Mark took the signal and followed Jack up the rickety steps. When he reached the top of the stairs, Mark met the rest of Jack's family, his wife and two female kittens. Mark's eyes grew wide as he realized he had just found the perfect "father's surprise gift" for his two little girls.

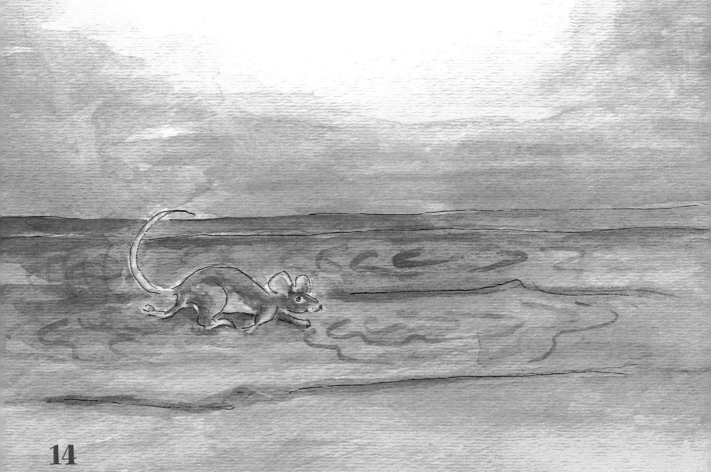

Jack and his family enjoyed the ride in the warm police cruiser. They meowed the whole way to the veterinarian in Mark's hometown. When Mark explained the story of how he found Jack and his family to Dr. Noodleman and his staff, they were eager to help with the Christmas Eve surprise. Dr. Noodleman's office made sure that Jack and his family were cleaned up, fluffed up and fed.

M ark went to the local pet store and bought cat food, cat litter and brand new Christmas kitty collars for Jack and his family. Then he went back to Dr. Noodleman's where his staff had decorated, in the finest of Christmas fashion, a big cardboard box with plenty of air and a comfy, warm quilt inside.

When Mark arrived home, Julie was thrilled to see that he was coming up the walkway with a big decorated box. She was fearful that he would come home empty-handed, having forgotten about their family tradition. When he came through the door, he smiled at his wife and gave her the biggest, jolliest "Merry Christmas" greeting.

Mark put the beautifully decorated box on the floor where his two daughters gathered around. He gently lifted the lid, and ever so slowly, Jack stood up on his hind legs to survey the room. To his delight, Mark lifted him out of the box. Jack's wife was whisked out by Julie and each of their daughters delighted in the warm embrace of a cute, cuddly kitten. For Mark's family, it was the best Christmas ever!

For Jack, it was the answer to his prayers.

Made in the USA
Middletown, DE
01 November 2017